For Maureen Poland – M.W.

To Bill and Irene – J.C.

ORCHARD BOOKS
96 Leonard Street, London EC2A 4XD
Hachette Children's Books
Level 17/207 Kent Street, Sydney, NSW 2000
First published in hardback in Great Britain in 2004
First paperback publication in 2005
ISBN 1 84362 014 6
Text © Martin Waddell 2004
Illustrations © Jason Cockcroft 2004
The rights of Martin Waddell to be identified as the author and Jason Cockcroft to
be identified as the illustrator of this work have been asserted by them in
accordance with the Copyright, Designs and Patents Act, 1988.
A CIP catalogue record for this book is available from the British Library.
1 3 5 7 9 10 8 6 4 2
Printed in Singapore

Room for a Little One

Martin Waddell

Illustrated by Jason Cockcroft

ORCHARD BOOKS

It was a cold winter's night.
Kind Ox lay in his stable,
close to the side of the inn.

Old Dog came by.

He stopped, and looked into the stable.

"I need somewhere to rest," said Old Dog.

"Come inside," Kind Ox said.

"There's always room for a little one here."

Old Dog came in and lay down in the straw.

He nestled close to Kind Ox,

sharing the warmth of his stable.

Stray Cat peered in.

She saw Old Dog and she stopped.

Stray Cat arched her back and her fur bristled.

"I'll not chase you," said Old Dog.

"Come inside," Kind Ox said.

"There's always room for a little one here."

Stray Cat came into the stable.

She curled up in the straw,

close to the friends she had found,

purring and twitching her tail.

Small Mouse stopped at the door of the stable.

She saw Stray Cat and she quivered with fear.

"You're safe here, I won't harm you," said Stray Cat.

"Come inside," Kind Ox said.

"There's always room for a little one here."

Small Mouse scurried in.

She nestled down warm in the straw,

in the peace of the stable.

Then Tired Donkey came.

Joseph led him along.

Mary rode on Tired Donkey's back.

Joseph was cold and Mary was weary,

but there was no room at the inn.

"Where will my baby be born?" Mary asked.

"Come inside," Kind Ox called to Tired Donkey.

"There's always room for a little one here."

Tired Donkey brought Mary into the stable.
Joseph made her a warm bed in the straw,
to save her from the cold of the night.

And so Jesus was born with the animals around Him;
Kind Ox, Old Dog, Stray Cat, Small Mouse, and
Tired Donkey all welcomed Him to the
warmth of their stable.

That cold winter's night,
beneath the star's light …

…a Little One came for the world.

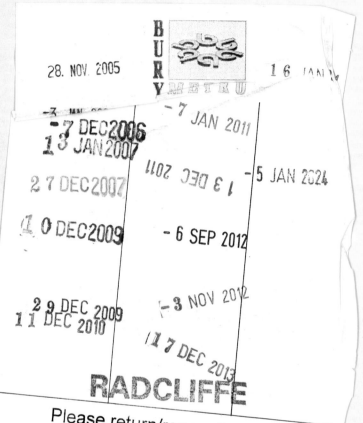

B U R Y METRO

28. NOV. 2005   16 JAN 20

-3 JAN   - 7 JAN 2011

-7 DEC 2006
13 JAN 2007

2 7 DEC 2007   1 3 DEC 2011   -5 JAN 2024

1 0 DEC 2009   - 6 SEP 2012

2 9 DEC 2009   - 3 NOV 2012
1 1 DEC 2010

1 7 DEC 2013

RADCLIFFE

Please return/renew this item
by the last date shown.
Books may also be renewed by
phone or the Internet.

www.bury.gov.uk/libraries